We, but Me

A Book for Twins
(or Any Two Peas in a Pod)

Written by Kenny Lee
Illustrated by Kai-Hua Cheng

To Angela, Jordyn, and Zoie, who inspire me daily. And to Taka and Nhan, for bringing out the best in any kid.

— K.L.

To Matt and Drake, for their love and support on my creative journey.

— K-H.C.

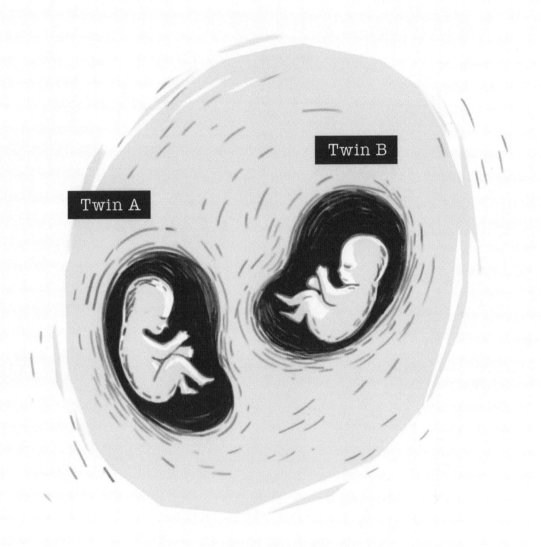

Two unique souls.
United by birth.

We share the same birthday,

but we were born minutes apart.

We have the same last name,

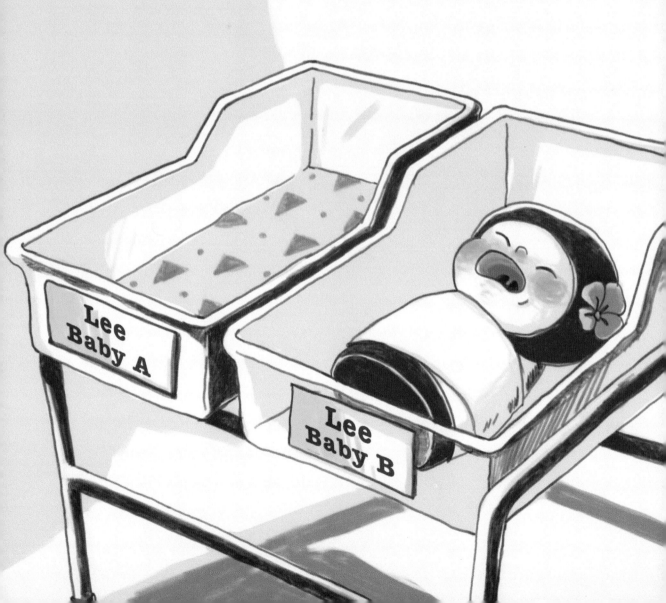

but our first names are distinct.

We might look alike,

We sleep in the same room,

but we have our own beds.

We both adore teddy bears,

but one size doesn't fit all.

We fight over the same toys,

but we share now and then.

We wear matching outfits,

but not every day.

We could get mistaken for one another,

but that can be fun.

We know the same kids,

but we play with our own friends.

We both love a good treat,

but we have different tastes.

We'll always be twins,

but we still get to be
you and me.

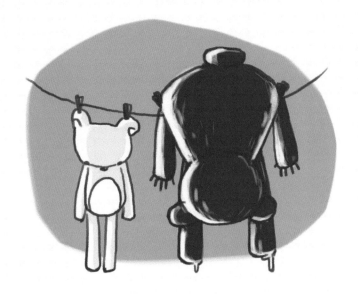

Book design by Kai-Hua Cheng.
The text of this book is set in Skippy Sharp and American Typewriter.
The illustrations were created using Adobe Photoshop CC.
Published in Pacifica, California.

Library of Congress Control Number: 2018913627
ISBN: 978-1-7325435-1-5
First edition 2019

This is Kenny's first book, and it was written to honor his twin girls. When Kenny isn't staring at a blank computer screen trying to write the next thing, he's a creative director in advertising and marketing. Originally from New Jersey, Kenny lives south of the Golden Gate Bridge with his wife and daughters.

Kai-Hua has a graduate degree in narrative illustration from Haute école des arts du Rhin in Strasbourg, France. More than a visual designer for a tech firm, Kai-Hua is also a painter, a graphic designer, and a linguist. And for fun, she likes to learn different musical instruments. Kai-Hua lives north of the Golden Gate Bridge with her husband and son.

Printed in Great Britain
by Amazon

84496048R00020